The
Good Giants
and the
Bad Pukwudgies

by
Jean Fritz

illustrated by
Tomie de Paola

G.P. Putnam's Sons
New York

To Jim, an active pukwudgie.
—J.F.

For my cousin, Mary Downey Malavese.
—T. deP.

Text copyright © 1982 by Jean Fritz
Illustrations copyright © 1982 by Tomie dePaola
All rights reserved.
Published simultaneously in Canada.
Sandcastle Books and the Sandcastle logo
are trademarks belonging to the Putnam & Grosset Group.
Printed in the United States of America.
First Sandcastle Books edition, 1989
Library of Congress Cataloging in Publication Data
Fritz, Jean.
The good giants and the bad pukwudgies.
Summary: The giant Maushop and his family
form the geography of Cape Cod in their battles
with the pukwudgies.
1. Wampanoag Indians–Legends. 2. Indians
of North America–Massachusetts–Legends.
[1. Wampanoag Indians–Legends. 2. Indians
of North America–Massachusetts–Legends.
3. Cape Cod (Mass.)–Fiction] 1. De Paola,
Tomie, ill. II. Title.
E99.W2F74 398.2'09'744'92 [398.2] [E] 81-17921
ISBN 0-399-20870-4 (hardcover)
ISBN 0-399-21732-0 (paperback)
First impression (hardcover)
First Sandcastle Books impression

There once was and there still is a narrow land that darts off from the coast of America as if it were running away from home. Long ago the First People lived here and beside them lived magic folk, good and bad both.

There were good giants: Maushop, his wife Quant, and their five giant sons. And there were bad pukwudgies: small, sly, ugly, and mean.

The First People went about their business—fishing, planting corn, picking berries, raising babies, and dancing on the beach.

And the pukwudgies went about their business— plotting mischief, contriving tricks, and concocting villainies. Sometimes they'd pull up a whole cornfield just for the fun of dressing up in corn silk. Then they'd prance around, la-de-da-ing and laughing themselves silly. Afterward, they would string their little oaken bows and their tiny finger-length arrows and they'd practice shooting high. Ping!

Sometimes they turned themselves into mosquitoes just to see how fast they could break up a beach dance. When the dancers would run ow-ing and yow-ing for home, the pukwudgies would become pukwudgies again. They'd grin their wicked grins and wipe the blood from their lips. Afterward, they would string their oaken bows and practice shooting high. Ping!

Sometimes they changed into fireflies on a dark night. They'd hide along a trail, their lights off, until some boys came their way. Then they'd light up and zigzag, flitter-flutter until they had led those boys far off the trail. Right into a mucky, sticky, soggy swamp. Then the pukwudgies would become pukwudgies again. They'd giggle their mean giggles and make nasty, slurpy, glug-glug noises like a swamp swallowing. Afterward, they would string their oaken bows and practice shooting high. Ping!

When the pukwudgies became so bad that the First People couldn't stand them one minute longer, they'd call on Maushop the Giant for help. Now, Maushop was good but he was lazy. What he liked most was to sit cross-legged on the beach and smoke his pipe. He'd puff up great clouds of smoke and let them drift foglike and lazy over the Narrow Land. The First People would smile. Old Maushop was at it again, they would say. Smoking his head off.

One day after an especially long and hard spell with
the pukwudgies, the First People went to Maushop. They
could barely see him for the smoke but they nudged his
feet and shouted.

"The pukwudgies!" they cried. "Time to give them a
good shake-up!"

Maushop blew a smoke ring out over the ocean. Well,
well, he'd attend to it, he sighed. He tilted his head back
and blew a ring around the sun. As soon as he finished
his pipe, he said.

Three days later Maushop had smoked his pipe down to the last bit of pokeweed. He tamped it out, stuck it in his belt, and when the smoke had lifted, he set out, pukwudgie-hunting. From one end of the Narrow Land to the other he stomped, shaking pukwudgies out of trees, scooping them out of bushes, scraping them off beaches. As soon as he had a handful, he shook them up until they rattled; then he tossed them sky-high. Up they went and down they tumbled, landing THUD all over the Narrow Land. Everyone knew, of course, that this was not the end of the pukwudgies. But at least it quieted them down for a time.

Old Maushop was worn out when he'd finished, so he stretched his full length along the south shore of the Narrow Land and fell asleep. His feet stuck up like pillars at one end of the land; his head lay like a boulder at the other. But he was restless. He twisted this way and turned that way in his sleep, so that by morning he'd dug out a bay at one end of the land and heaved up cliffs at the other end. Moreover, he'd filled his moccasins with sand.

The first thing Maushop did when he woke up was take off those moccasins. He stood up and flung the sand from one moccasin into the sea. Where the sand landed, an island sprang up. Then he flung the sand from the other moccasin into the sea. And there was another island. Maushop smiled. Those were good islands, he thought. He'd just sit down, have a smoke, and look them over. But when he reached into his belt for his pipe, it wasn't there.

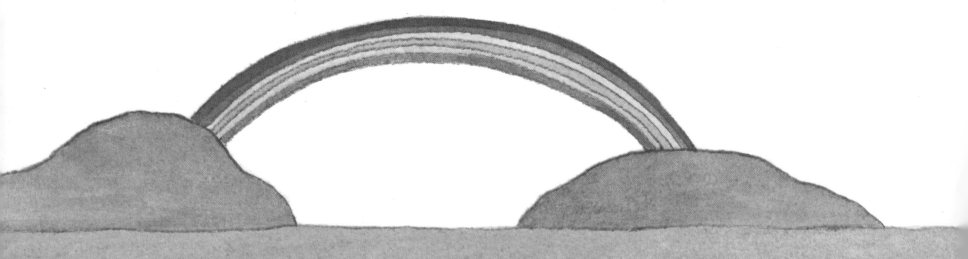

Instead, standing before him was his wife, Quant. Sticking out of her hand was the stem of his pipe.

"No smoking today," Quant said. "Work to do. Hoeing. Weeding. Don't know what-all."

Maushop sighed. He hated hoeing and weeding and he didn't like the sound of what-all.

"Where are the boys?" he asked.

"Off."

Off whaling, Maushop supposed. That was the trouble with boys, he thought. Good as they were, they went off.

"Well, let the work wait," Maushop said, but he knew he was wasting words. When Quant said it was a working day, that's what it was.

Quant strode down the beach. "Strawberries be ripe," she called over her shoulder.

Without another word, Maushop followed Quant home. If the strawberries were ripe, Quant would bake. And there was nothing in this wide world that Maushop doted on more than Quant's fresh strawberry bread.

So every day during strawberry season, Maushop
hoed and weeded and took care of what-all and every
evening he gorged himself on Quant's strawberry bread.
When at last the strawberries petered out, Maushop
filled a bag with pokeweed, tucked his pipe into his belt,
and set off for the beach. When he got there, he took
off his moccasins, tied the laces together, slung the
moccasins over his shoulder, and waded out to the first
of those two islands he'd made for himself.

It was a grand little island. No pukwudgies on it. No crops. No one to bother him. Maushop found a fine cliff at the far end of the island, sat down cross-legged, and lit his pipe. He puffed up his cheeks and blew out great billows of smoke; he tightened his jaw and let smoke dribble out of his mouth, wisp by wisp. He funneled smoke out through his ears and squirted it out through his nose. All the smoke rolled bleary and foglike to the Narrow Land.

Then one morning as Maushop was sitting cross-legged on his clifftop, a song floated up to him, the likes of which he had never heard before. A thin little rippling tune it was, skipping through the spray. A trill that wound its way, secretlike, out of a seashell. Teasing. Coaxing. Promising. And wet.

With one giant step Maushop was off the cliff and down on the beach, but whatever direction he turned, the song seemed to bubble up from somewhere behind him.

Maushop strode into the water. "Where are you? And what are you?" he shouted.

At first he thought he heard only his echo. From far out at sea came an underwater booming that sounded like his own voice. Then the booming burst into a waterfall of laughter and he knew it was a singer, mocking him.

Maushop didn't know what to do next. So he decided to go home.

The thought had hardly crossed his mind, however, when a great storm blew up between the island and the Narrow Land. Waves thrashed about and lightning crisscrossed the sky. It lasted only a few minutes and when it was over, Maushop heard the singer's voice, liquid and larky, right beside him.

"I did that," the voice said, proud. Sitting on a rock by his feet was a woman dressed in seaweed with long green ribbons of hair streaming down her back. She had square eyes and webbed hands and she was laughing. "I'm Squant," she said. "A sea woman."

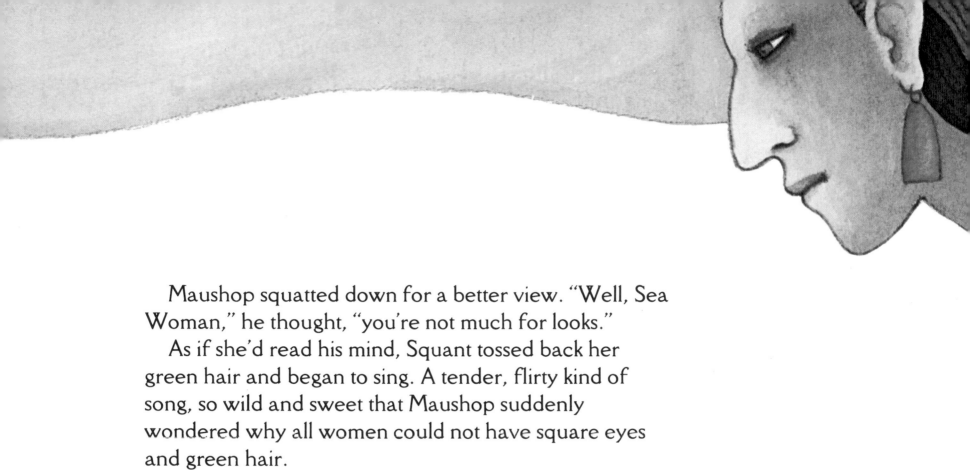

Maushop squatted down for a better view. "Well, Sea Woman," he thought, "you're not much for looks."

As if she'd read his mind, Squant tossed back her green hair and began to sing. A tender, flirty kind of song, so wild and sweet that Maushop suddenly wondered why all women could not have square eyes and green hair.

He shifted uneasily on the sand. "Why did you make the storm?" he asked.

"I don't want you to go home." Squant twirled the bracelet of jingle shells on her arm. "I want someone to play with in the water." She laughed a tinkly laugh and scooping up a handful of water, she blew it into bubbles. "I doubt you even know how to swim," she scoffed.

Maushop could see that he didn't even know how to talk to people who swam. "I have no need to swim," he said stiffly. "I am a land person and tall. I wade."

"But you don't know the fun!" Squant began to hum in such a dancing-daring kind of way that Maushop found it hard to keep his feet still.

Then she grabbed his hand and before Maushop knew what he was doing, he was leaping through the waves, cavorting out to the open sea, swooping under water, bouncing back, romping as he never knew it was possible to romp, laughing as he never dreamed he could laugh.

"You see? You see?" Squant laughed and splashed him in the face.

"I see." Maushop laughed and splashed her back.

Once it began, so it went, day after day, frolicking in and out of the water, over and under waves. Squant taught Maushop how to play leapfrog with the porpoises. She showed him castles on the floor of the ocean. She introduced him to creeping and crawling things he would never have believed, had he not seen for himself.

Sometimes Maushop glanced over at the Narrow Land and it looked lonesome to him. And he thought, "Enough is enough," and he'd start for home. But let him take a single step and Squant would let loose a long silken thread of a song that would catch him in its web. Then back he'd be, playing tag, somersaulting through the breakers. He lost all track of time, from one day to another, from one month to the next. He didn't think of his pipe which he'd left on the clifftop when the singing had begun. He didn't wonder about the pukwudgies or even guess how bold they might have grown while he was away.

Then one morning while Squant was on the beach, untangling her green hair and braiding it, Maushop smelled a familiar smell drifting over from the Narrow Land. Strawberry bread, that's what it was. Maushop stole a glance at Squant. She'd found a mirror-pool in the rocks and she was turning her head this way and smiling, then turning it that way and smiling. She was too taken with herself to think of anything else. So, quietly Maushop reached up to the cliff for his pipe, tucked it into his belt, and making his feet slippery-silent, he waded to the Narrow Land.

On the shore his five giant sons were waiting for him.

" 'Bout time you came home," the oldest one grumbled. "The pukwudgies have gone daft."

Maushop looked at his sons, all of them wanderers, none of them pipe-smokers. "Well, why didn't you take care of them?" he snapped.

The five boys shook their heads. "Couldn't do it, Pa. Not without you." The oldest one spoke for them all.

It was provoking, Maushop thought. Five big boys able to go off whenever it suited their fancy but couldn't handle the first bit of home-trouble.

"Well, why didn't you come for me then?"

"Couldn't do it, Pa. Every time we started, a storm rose up."

Maushop sighed. "So what foolishness are the pukwudgies up to now?"

The five boys shook their heads. "Not foolishness. Deviltry."

"Setting fire to thatched roofs."

"Pushing men off cliffs."

"Running off with papooses."

Well, that was very bad, Maushop agreed. "We'll go eat some of your Ma's strawberry bread," he said, "and then we'll go a-hunting."

Again the boys shook their heads.

"Can't do it, Pa," the oldest son said. "They stole the strawberry bread."

"They WHAT?" Maushop brushed aside his sons and strode into the hut where Quant had her arms deep into a new batch of pink dough.

"They stole your bread?" Maushop shouted.

Quant looked at him squinty-eyed as if it were all his fault. "Two loaves," she snapped. She kneaded, slapped, and punched the new dough.

"Come on, boys," Maushop roared. "We're going now!"

Maushop planned to go to the far end of the land and sent the five boys to the middle part where the tall grasses grew. "Best to lie down in the grass," Maushop advised, "so you can see better."

Peeping out from bushes, listening from treetops, the pukwudgies choked back their fiendish laughter and scurried through the shadows to the tall grassy place. When the five giant boys arrived, the pukwudgies were already there. Over their shoulders hung their oaken bows. Tight in their fists they held magic sand. As soon as the boys flopped belly-down in the grass, the pukwudgies threw that magic sand right into their eyes so they couldn't see a thing.

Howling, the giants leaped to their feet. Stumbling. Groping. Calling back and forth. Rubbing their eyes.

"Look at the sun!" the oldest cried. "See, can you catch any light from it?"

As soon as the giants stood still and raised their blind
eyes to the sun, those pukwudgies did just what they'd
been practicing all this while. They strung their oaken
bows with poisoned arrows and they shot high. Right at
the giants' hearts. Ping, ping, ping, ping, and ping! Like
great trees in the forest, the giants fell, crashing to the
ground with a thunder that set the land shuddering from
one end to the other.

Quant had just begun to bake a loaf of bread when she heard the boys fall. Maushop was down-island, scouring the sand dunes for pukwudgie tracks when he heard. Both rushed to the grassy place, knocking down trees that stood in their way, plunging through swamps as if they were no more than rain puddles. They both reached the grassy place at the same time. And there were their five good sons, lying in a row like logs, waiting to be hauled away.

Roaring and wailing, the two stamped furiously all over the grassy place, crushing pukwudgies beneath their feet, catching them in their hands and squeezing them until their eyes popped out. Running every which way, the pukwudgies tripped over each other as they tried to escape. Some got away, but many ended up as holes in the ground.

Maushop's and Quant's rage finally eased and gave way to grief. Tears streaming down their cheeks, they carried their sons, one by one, and buried them at sea. Laid out in the water, the five sons became five islands, long whalelike islands, their backs humped.

"I guess they'd like it that way," Maushop sighed as the two waded back to the Narrow Land.

Quant went into the hut and came out with a fresh loaf of strawberry bread. The fact that five boys could be killed while a loaf of bread was baking was a hard thing to think on. But the bread was there, ready for eating, so she put it on a mat. She and Maushop sat on either side and ate.

After a while Quant spoke. "Know what I'm thinking?" she said. "It'll take more than burying to keep those boys from running off."

Maushop sat up straighter. "Maybe so." He took a hunk of bread and chewed on it thoughtfully. "No reason why they shouldn't go. Every once in a while. Like old times. Some dark night when no one's looking, they can take a run down the coast or out to sea."

"Won't nobody know the difference," Quant agreed. "You fill the air with that pipe smoke of yours and no telling what they'll be up to."

Maushop smiled. "No telling." As soon as the last crumb of strawberry bread was gone, he lit his pipe. He blew great banks of thick, yellow, foglike smoke over the five islands. When the smoke began to thin out, Maushop covered the islands again.

People didn't see much of Quant and Maushop after that. Pretty soon New People who didn't understand magic moved to the Narrow Land. They talked about fog rolling in, not thinking a giant might be smoking his pipe. They complained about mosquitoes breaking up their beach parties, not guessing that pukwudgies were just having their fun.

So over the years people come and people go, often
as not, blind to what's really going on. But magic stays.
Same as always, it's there, likely at the bottom of
everything. Good and bad magic, both.

NOTE

The Narrow Land is really Cape Cod. The First People were the Wampanoag tribe of the Algonquin Indians who told stories about Maushop and Quant and their five sons, about the bad pukwudgies, and about Squant, the Sea Woman. The bay that Maushop hollowed out in his sleep, according to the Wampanoags, is Buzzards Bay. The two islands formed from the sand in his moccasins are Martha's Vineyard and Nantucket. The five island graves of the giant sons are the Elizabeth Islands.

I have combined fragments of old legends collected by Elizabeth Reynard in a fine book called THE NARROW LAND. I have retained basic events and characters, but I have adapted and added dialogue and scenes, telling the story as Maushop might tell it today. And if he's picked up some Yankee speech in all these years, what else would you expect?